D0105806

DISCARDED
CONCORD PUBLIC LIBRARY
45 GREEN STREET
CONCORD, NH 03301

The Case of the Tortoise in Trouble

The Case of the Tortoise in Trouble

BY NANCY KRULIK

ILLUSTRATED BY GARY LaCOSTE

SCHOLASTIC INC.
New York Toronto London Auckland
Sydney Mexico City New Delhi Hong Kong

For Ian, keeper of the family tortoise

If you purchased this book without a cover, you should be aware that this book is stolen property. It was reported as "unsold and destroyed" to the publisher, and neither the author nor the publisher has received any payment for this "stripped book."

No part of this publication may be reproduced, stored in a retrieval system, or transmitted in any form or by any means, electronic, mechanical, photocopying, recording, or otherwise, without written permission of the publisher. For information regarding permission, write to Scholastic Inc., Attention: Permissions Department, 557 Broadway, New York, NY 10012.

ISBN 978-0-545-26655-0

Text copyright © 2011 by Nancy Krulik
Illustrations copyright © 2011 by Scholastic Inc.
All rights reserved. Published by Scholastic Inc.
SCHOLASTIC and associated logos are trademarks
and/or registered trademarks of Scholastic Inc.

12 11 10 9 8 7 6 5 4 3 11 12 13 14 15 16/0

Printed in the U.S.A. 40
First printing, July 2011
Book design by Yaffa Jaskoll

Chapter 1

"Can I go on your field trip? Please, Jack! I've never been to a farm. I wanna go. Please!"

I was sitting at the breakfast table, getting ready to scarf down a blueberry pancake, when my pet beagle, Scout, started barking in my face.

To everyone else in my family, it just sounded like Scout was begging for people food instead of dog food. But I knew what was really going on. That's because I can talk to animals. *Really.* I understand them. And they understand me.

It all started a few weeks ago when I got hit by an acorn from the big oak tree in my front yard. Ordinarily, the only thing an acorn bash to the head would have left me with is a lump. But this tree was a magic tree.

Seriously. If a human gets hit with an acorn from that tree, he gets special powers—like being able to talk to animals.

I didn't believe it at first. Who would? But it's true. Zippy and Zappy, the two squirrels who live in the tree, told me. And if you can't believe squirrels, who can you believe? They're pretty much the experts when it comes to acorns.

Anyhow, that's how I knew Scout was begging me to take him on my school field trip to the Oat Run Farm.

"Dogs aren't allowed on school trips," I explained to him.

"What?" My mother turned from the griddle and gave me a funny look.

Oops. I hadn't meant to talk to Scout in front of my family. I had never told my parents about the whole being-hit-with-an-acorn-and-talking-to-animals thing. They'd probably never let me go near a tree again as long as I lived. That's just how parents are.

"I meant to say, 'Dogs can't have pancakes,'" I said quickly. *Phew. Good save.*

My mother plopped a blueberry pancake on my five-year-old sister Mia's plate. "Breakfast is served," she said.

Mia looked down at her pancake and started counting. "Five, six, seven, eight." She shot me a nasty smile. "I bet that's more blueberries than you have, Jack."

I popped a whole pancake in my mouth. "Whatever."

"Jack's talking with his mouth full," Mia tattled.

My mother looked over. I swallowed really fast.

"I think that shirt's a little small," my mom told me.

I shrugged. "My Tigers shirt is my have-a-good-time-on-a-field-trip shirt," I said. "I have to wear it."

"Speaking of field trips, you must be looking forward to spending the day outdoors at the farm," my dad said.

"I wish *I* was going to a farm," Mia said. "I love animals. Especially my Tut."

Tut is Mia's desert tortoise. He lives in a terrarium in her room.

"I bet Tut would love to visit a farm," Mia continued.

Now *Mia* was talking with her mouth full. But I didn't say anything. I'm not a tattler. Besides, it was funny watching bits of purple pancake drip out of her mouth.

"Why don't you bring Tut with you on your field trip?" Mia asked me.

I shook my head. "I'm not bringing a tortoise to school."

"But you're not going to *be* in school," Mia said. "You're going to a farm. And Tut would love it. Don't you want him to be happy?"

"Why does everyone want to go on my field trip?" I groaned.

Mia gave me a strange look. "Who's everyone?" she wondered. "I just asked about Tut."

Oops. I'd almost blown it. Again. I couldn't let Mia the Pain know that I could talk to Scout—or any other animal. She'd tell everybody. Mia cannot keep a secret!

"I mean, I'm sure Scout would want to go run around on a farm, but I'm not bringing him," I said quickly. "And I'm not bringing Tut, either."

Mia scowled. I got ready for some major screaming or whining.

PLEASE PLEASE PLEASE
sigh
PLEASE PLEASE PLEASE

But Mia didn't say anything. She just shrugged and took another bite of her pancake.

Wow! Mia had given up. I'd won the battle. And it had been so easy!

But Scout wasn't giving up nearly as easily. He wanted to go to that farm really badly. I guess he figured if he barked loud enough I'd give in.

"Come on, Jack," Scout yelped. "I just want to go somewhere fun. Are you going to get to go in a car? Are you going to get to eat really good people food? You know I love people food."

I just drank my juice and tried to ignore him.

Actually, ignoring Scout was easy. But it was pretty hard to ignore what was going on outside the kitchen window. Two squirrels were busy making faces at me.

No, *really.* They were making faces. Zippy, the one with the bite in his ear, was sticking his tongue out at me. *"Na na na na na,"* he chattered. "You can't catch us." He turned around and wiggled his big squirrel butt right at me.

Zappy, his brother, was holding up his little paws and pretending to box. "Come on out, Big Head," he

said, using his stupid nickname for me. He punched the air—and fell backward right into the bushes.

"I meant to do that!" Zappy shouted.

I burst out laughing. I couldn't help it. Zippy and Zappy were real goofballs.

"Mommy!" Mia shouted out. "Jack's laughing at me!"

"I am not," I insisted. "I'm . . ."

Just then, a really bad stink filled the kitchen.

"Pee-yew," Mia said. "Who did that?"

"It wasn't me," I told her.

"It wasn't me, either," Mia said.

"She who smelt it, dealt it," I told my little sister.

"Are you calling me a liar?" Mia whined. "MOMMY!"

"I'm just saying—"

Suddenly, Scout interrupted me. "It was me," he whimpered. "I gotta go outside."

"I think Scout needs to go to the bathroom," I told my mom. "Is it okay if I take him for a quick walk before school?"

"Don't let me stop you," my mom said. "Get that stinky dog out of here."

Lucky me. Saved by the *smell*.

Chapter 2

"You ready for this trip?" the Brainiac asked me. She and I were standing outside the school building with the rest of the third graders, waiting for the buses that would take us to the farm.

Actually, the Brainiac's real name is Elizabeth. Everyone just calls her the Brainiac because she's the smartest girl in school.

"I guess." I looked down and tried not to notice the way Elizabeth was blinking and smiling at me.

"It's going to be tough for you with all those animals," she said.

"Shhh . . ." I warned. "There are people around."

Elizabeth is the only person in the whole world who knows about me being able to talk to animals. She heard me talking to Scout one morning when I didn't think anyone was around.

Lots of people have heard me say things like *sit*, or *stay*, or *roll over* to Scout. But that wasn't the kind of conversation Scout and I were having. And Elizabeth knew it. She figured out what was going on. She isn't called the Brainiac for nothing.

Luckily, Elizabeth is very good at keeping secrets. I really didn't want anyone else knowing I could talk to animals. They'd make fun of me. Especially Trevor the Terrible. He's a total jerk.

A total jerk heading right toward Elizabeth and me!

My palms got sweaty. Trevor's the biggest kid in our whole grade—and the meanest.

"Oh, look, it's the kissy faces, together again," Trevor said so loudly everyone could hear him.

Oh man. That made me mad. I do *not* like Elizabeth. At least not the way Trevor meant it!

"WE ARE NOT KISSY FACES!" I shouted so everyone could hear me, too.

"Then why are you always together?" Trevor asked.

"Because we're detectives," Elizabeth told him. "And

SCHOOL

partners." She twirled one of her wormy-looking red curls around her finger and gave me a smile.

I don't like when Elizabeth smiles at me that way. She makes it look like we really *are* kissy faces—which we most definitely are not!

"Oh, *right.*" Trevor laughed. He sounded like he didn't believe a word she was saying. *"Detectives."*

Trevor could laugh all he wanted, but Elizabeth and I really *were* detectives. We'd already solved our first case by finding my best friend Leo's plans for the science fair—with some help from Scout and his dog friends.

It turns out animals are really helpful when it comes to solving mysteries. Crooks don't usually worry about having animals as witnesses because they don't think animals can talk. Boy, are they wrong.

Trevor must have gotten bored teasing Elizabeth and me because he suddenly walked away—probably to find someone else to bother.

As soon as Trevor was gone, Leo walked over to us. Leo's the smallest kid in our grade, so Trevor seems *really* huge and scary next to him. I think that's why Leo stays as far away from Trevor as possible.

"You want to be my field-trip buddy?" Leo asked me.

"Definitely," I said. "Like always."

Elizabeth gave me a weird look and shifted her backpack onto her other shoulder. I got the feeling she thought *she* was going to be my buddy this time. Being detective partners is one thing. But being buddies on a school field trip is another.

Luckily, one girl in our class, Sasha, didn't have a buddy yet. She was really happy to have the Brainiac as a partner—especially because we had to work with our buddies to fill in a worksheet during the trip. Some worksheet questions can be pretty tough—for everyone but Elizabeth.

"Let's get on the bus first, so we can have our pick of seats," Sasha told Elizabeth. She spun around so fast her long brown braid nearly hit me in the face. "I like to sit near the back. How about you?"

Elizabeth shot me another look. It was kind of pitiful. I could tell she didn't want to be buddies with Sasha all day. Not that I blamed her. Sasha never stopped talking. And she was really loud.

But what could I do? Elizabeth and I may have been partners, but Leo was my buddy. My *best* buddy. That's just the way things were.

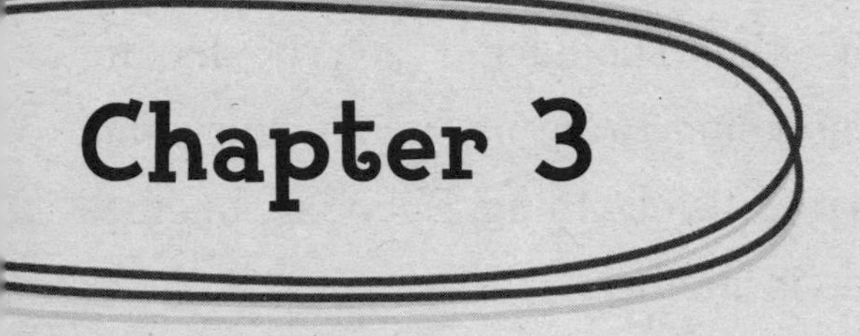

Chapter 3

"Do your ears hang low? Do they wobble to and fro?" I sang along with the other kids on my bus as we headed down the highway to the farm. I was feeling pretty good. *"Can you tie them in a knot? Can you tie them in a bow?"*

Suddenly, I glanced down at my backpack. It was squirming in the seat next to me. I did a double take. Backpacks aren't supposed to move, especially when all that's inside them is a notebook, pencils, and the peanut butter and jelly sandwich that my mom had packed for my lunch.

Weird.

"Hey! Who turned out the lights?" the backpack said.

Double weird. Pencils, notebooks, and peanut butter [illegible] talk, either.

But *animals* squirm. And they talk. At least to me. I reached into my bag and pulled out a very frightened tortoise.

"Tut! Oh, Mia!" I shouted out angrily.

"Why did you bring Mia's tortoise?" Leo asked me. "He's going to ruin our whole day."

"I didn't—" I began.

"I could have brought my guinea pig, Mr. Sniffles," Leo interrupted. "But I didn't."

"*I* didn't bring Tut, either," I told him. "Mia must have shoved him into my backpack. I should have known. She gave in way too easily this morning."

Mrs. Sloane looked back to see what the commotion was about. "Jack! What is that?"

"My sister's tortoise," I explained.

"Why would you bring a tortoise on a field trip?" Mrs. Sloane asked me. She sounded angry. Not that I blamed her. I was angry, too.

"I didn't," I said.

Trevor started to laugh. "Uh, hello? You're holding a tortoise right now."

Everyone on the bus giggled.

Grrr . . . Trevor can be such a jerk.

"Trevor does have a point," Mrs. Sloane told me. "Do you mind explaining this?"

"I didn't bring Tut on purpose," I insisted. "My sister must have snuck him into my backpack when I wasn't looking."

"Your sister shouldn't have a tortoise for a pet," Sasha said. "Tortoises aren't supposed to live in glass cages. They're supposed to live free in . . . well . . . wherever they're from."

"He's a desert tortoise," I said.

"In a desert, then." Sasha pushed her glasses back up on her nose, flipped her long braid behind her, and folded her arms over her purple T-shirt. Now *she* looked angry, too.

Oh great. So now there were four people who were upset because of the tortoise—Leo, Mrs. Sloane, Sasha, and, of course, me. Pretty soon the only person who wasn't going to be angry was Trevor—because he liked making fun of me for having a tortoise in my backpack.

I didn't want to argue with Sasha. I just wanted to figure out what I was going to do with Tut.

Luckily, Mrs. Sloane had an idea. When we got to the farm, she found a box for Tut and then got a bowl of water from the manager of the farm.

"We'll leave Tut with our lunches in the red barn," Mrs. Sloane told me. "It's warm enough for him to be comfortable, and the barn door is open for him to get some fresh air."

"How come there aren't any windows in this box?" Tut asked. "My other box had a great view."

A view of Mia's messy room, I thought. But I didn't say that out loud. The last thing I needed was for Mrs. Sloane to find out I could talk to animals.

Instead, I just said, "Thanks, Mrs. Sloane."

Mrs. Sloane shot me a smile almost as nice as the ones she usually gave to her favorite student, Trevor. "I have a little sister, too," she said. "They can be pains sometimes."

Sometimes? Mia was a pain *all* the time. But I wasn't going to let her ruin my day.

Chapter 4

"What's that stink?" Trevor the Terrible shouted as we walked into the big red barn.

"It's the animals," Elizabeth told him. "Their fur smells, and so does their . . . well . . . you know. When they go the bathroom."

Everyone laughed. Elizabeth's face got so red it matched her wormy, curly hair.

"I think the stink is coming from *Cubby's* backpack," Trevor said. He walked over and sniffed at Leo.

Now it was Leo's chance to turn red. Cubby was his mom's nickname for him—because Leo was a lion name and lion babies are cubs. The last thing Leo wanted was for everyone in school to know his nickname. But Trevor had heard Leo's mom say it once, and now he used it whenever he could.

But Trevor wasn't kidding about Leo's backpack. It smelled sometimes. Mostly because Leo usually forgot to throw out his leftover lunch.

"What's so funny?" Mrs. Sloane asked us.

"Oh, I was just telling farm jokes," Trevor said. He gave our teacher a big, fake smile.

"Getting everyone in the mood, Trevor?" she asked. "How terrific!"

I don't know why Mrs. Sloane falls for Trevor's nice-guy act. But she does. Every time.

Trevor smiled at her. Then he glared at Leo and me, just to make sure we weren't going to tell Mrs. Sloane what had really been going on.

We filed into the barn and sat down on big hay bales. Mrs. Sloane placed Tut's box on a shelf near the back of the barn.

"Welcome to the Oat Run Farm, boys and girls!" a man with a long gray beard and huge cowboy hat said as he walked into the barn. "I'm Mr. Trotter, and I manage this farm. Today, you're all junior farmhands. And to help you get into your new roles, here are your official farmhand hats."

Bzzz

Mrs. Sloane and the other two third-grade teachers began to hand out kid-size cowboy hats. They looked just like the one Mr. Trotter was wearing, except his was brown leather and ours were felt.

"Thanks," I said as Mrs. Sloane gave me one of the cowboy hats. It was pretty cool.

"Okay, kids," Mrs. Sloane said. "Now that you are all official junior farmhands, it's time to have fun. For the next half hour, I want you to check out the farm. Learn your way around. There are signs pointing to all the different places you can go. Check out the reptile room, and visit the dairy barn for a milking demonstration."

"There's also a petting zoo," Mr. Trotter suggested.

"Petting zoos are cruel," Sasha said loudly. "How do we know those animals even want to be petted? Did anyone ask them?"

"How are we supposed to do that?" Trevor asked her. "It's not like we speak goat or donkey."

Elizabeth looked over in my direction and giggled.

Oh man. Did she have to do that in front of people?

"You can go anywhere you want, Sasha," said Mrs. Ellery, another third-grade teacher. "Just remember to stick with your buddy, and answer questions on your worksheet about all the places you visit on the farm."

"And stay inside the yellow fences," Mr. Trotter told us. "We don't want anybody wandering."

"Each class will have a separate time for horseback riding. My students will be meeting at the stables at ten o'clock," Mrs. Sloane said. "Please don't be late."

A lot of people cheered for the horseback riding. But not me. I had something else on my mind.

Leo looked at me. "Dude, aren't you happy to be here?" he asked.

"Sure," I said. "I'm just worried about leaving Tut."

"Who cares about that stupid tortoise?" Leo asked.

"I have to care," I said. "Mia will kill me if anything happens to him."

"That tortoise is going to ruin our trip," Leo said. "You'll be thinking about him all day."

"No, I won't," I promised.

Leo gave me a look. I could tell he wasn't so sure.

"Where do you want to go first?" I asked, trying to sound like I'd forgotten Tut already.

"To the bathroom," Leo admitted. "All that bumping up and down on the bus made me have to go."

I laughed. "Okay. I'll meet you in the reptile room."

"Sounds like a plan," my buddy agreed. "It's always important to have a plan."

"Whoa, check out these snakes!" Leo said a few minutes later in the reptile room. "They're *huge*."

A woman walked over. Her nametag read AGGIE.

"These snakes were found on the farm," Aggie said. "That one's a northern red-bellied snake."

I reached into my backpack and pulled out my worksheet. *Yuck!* There was a small spot of brown and white goo at the bottom of the paper.

"Ewww," I groaned. "Tut pooped in my backpack!"

I grabbed a tissue from a shelf and wiped off the poop. Then I got a closer look at the snake. "What are you *ssss*taring at?" the snake hissed.

"Those stripes are neat looking," Leo said.

I wrote *reddish brown with four stripes* on the description part of the worksheet.

“Hey, you got any worm*ssss* or cricket*ssss*?” the snake asked me. “I’m *ssss*tarving.”

“When do you feed this snake?” I asked Aggie.

“In the morning,” Aggie replied. “He had a huge breakfast today—three crickets and an earthworm.”

“What a pig,” I said with a laugh.

“I’m not a pig. I’m a *ssss*nake,” he told me. “You two-leggeds are really *ssss*tupid.”

Talking about food had made me thirsty.

“I’m gonna run back to the red barn for a juice box,” I told Leo.

"Can't you wait?" Leo asked me. "I wanted to help collect the eggs from the chicken coop."

"I could just meet you there," I suggested. "The barn's not far from the coop. I'll be quick."

"Okay," Leo agreed. "Can you bring me one, too?"

"Sure thing!" I said.

I hurried over to barn and pulled out two very berry juice boxes from the cooler. Then, since I was there, I figured I'd check on Tut.

I walked over to the small haystack near the back of the barn. Tut's box was on the shelf beside it, just where we'd left it. There was only one problem.

Tut was missing!

Chapter 5

This was bad. *Really* bad. I was going to be in big trouble. It didn't matter that it wasn't my fault. Mia the Pain was definitely going to make sure I paid for this. I had to do something.

So I ran. As fast as I could.

I needed to find the Brainiac! I had to tell her that we had a mystery on our hands. A big one!

Luckily, Elizabeth wasn't far away. She was in the dairy barn with a bunch of other kids who had gone there to see the milking demonstration.

Okay. Now all I had to do was figure out a way to actually talk to Elizabeth in private. It wasn't going to be easy. Elizabeth wasn't just watching a cow being milked. She was actually doing the *milking.*

Sasha was crouching down and holding the milk pail, while Elizabeth pulled on those faucet-looking things underneath the cow's belly. Elizabeth seemed to be having a good time. Sasha did *not*.

"How do you know that cow wants to share its milk with us?" Sasha asked the farmhand. "You're stealing her milk. I bet she could have you arrested. I'm not going to hold this bucket. I'm not going to be a criminal."

I rolled my eyes. Sasha was such a drama queen.

"Actually, if we don't milk her she might be in pain," the farmhand said.

Sasha crossed her arms and glared.

As the farmhand explained how important milking was, I went over to Elizabeth. "I'll hold the bucket," I said, pushing my way up front.

"What are you doing here, Jack?" Elizabeth asked. Then she looked behind me. "And where's Leo?"

"I need to talk to you," I told Elizabeth.

"So you don't really want to help me milk the cow?" Elizabeth asked.

I shook my head. "It looks kind of gross."

“The udders are all wrinkly and warm,” Elizabeth admitted. “And Bessie stinks.”

Elizabeth wasn’t kidding. I’d never been that close to a cow before. Bessie smelled worse than Scout when he came in from the rain. And that was saying something.

“Will you *mooo*ve a little faster, please?” Bessie mooed loudly. “The sooner we fill this bucket with milk, the sooner I can go back to the pasture.”

“Bessie wants you to milk faster,” I whispered to Elizabeth.

Elizabeth pulled harder on the wrinkly pink udders. Milk squirted out into the bucket.

“That’s better,” Bessie mooed. “This may be fun for you. But for me, it’s just *an udder* day.”

“I’ve got a problem,” I whispered to Elizabeth. “I need your help.”

“Can’t Leo help you?” Elizabeth asked. “He’s your buddy, *remember*?”

I didn’t know why Elizabeth was mad about me picking Leo as a buddy. But right now I couldn’t fight with her. I needed her brain too badly.

"Leo doesn't solve mysteries," I whispered.

Elizabeth's eyes opened wide. "What mystery?" she asked.

"It's my sister's tortoise," I said. "He's disappeared."

Elizabeth was so surprised she almost fell off her stool. Her hand twitched excitedly.

SQUIRT! A big glob of warm milk squirted me right in the face.

"Yuck!" I wiped the milk out of my eyes. "That's disgusting."

"Don't be r*uuuu*de," Bessie mooed angrily. "My milk is the tastiest on the whole farm. You're lucky to try some fresh."

I didn't feel lucky. I felt like someone who was missing a tortoise and smelled like warm milk. "Come on," I said to Elizabeth. "We've gotta get on this case."

Elizabeth looked up at the farmhand. "Maybe someone else wants to try milking the cow," she suggested.

"I'll do it," Trevor said. "I'll bet I can fill that bucket faster than Elizabeth."

"Good for you, Trevor," Mrs. Sloane said. "I like when students volunteer. How about I hold the bucket for you?"

SQUIRT!

I wanted to tell Mrs. Sloane that I had volunteered to take Sasha's place just a minute before, but there was no point. Trevor was just Mrs. Sloane's favorite.

Meanwhile, Elizabeth had already jumped right into detective mode. She grabbed her backpack and pulled me away from the milking demonstration. We went over to a bench under a tree, where we could talk without anyone hearing us.

"Here, hold this," she said, reaching into her backpack and handing me a yellow sock. "And these," she added, handing me a glow-in-the-dark bandage, a stopwatch, and a clothespin.

"You carry the weirdest stuff," I told her.

"I like to be ready for any emergency," she said.

"This is *definitely* an emergency," I told her.

"We'll solve this mystery," Elizabeth promised me. She pulled her notebook out of her backpack and opened it to a fresh page. Elizabeth and I were now officially *on the case.*

Chapter 6

"Where's my juice box?"

I jumped off the bench when I heard Leo's voice. In all the missing-tortoise mess, I'd forgotten why I'd gone to the red barn in the first place. Leo had probably been waiting at the chicken coop for a while before he came looking for me.

"Sorry," I apologized. "I forgot all about meeting you when I realized something horrible had happened."

"What?" Leo asked. He sounded really worried.

"Tut's *missing*," I said.

Leo didn't seem so worried anymore. "I knew that tortoise was going to ruin things," he grumbled.

"It'll be okay as soon as we find him," Elizabeth promised.

"We?" Leo repeated. "You mean *you* and Jack?"

"Of course," Elizabeth said. "I'm his detective partner." She moved a little closer to me and smiled.

I moved a little farther from her and frowned.

"Forget it," Leo said angrily. "I'll get my own juice. I'll meet you at the stables for horseback riding—if you can get away from your mystery long enough to ride."

"We'll be there," I promised.

"Okay," Elizabeth said as Leo walked away. "Let's get started. What do we know so far?"

"Not much," I admitted. "Just that Tut is missing. I don't even know if he escaped or if he was stolen."

"I'm sure he was stolen," Elizabeth said. "A tortoise has short legs. Even if Tut escaped from his box, he never could have climbed down from the shelf."

That was true. But there was no reason for Elizabeth to be acting so proud of herself. It didn't take a Brainiac to figure out a tortoise can't climb down from a high shelf. I would have thought of it, eventually.

"The question is, *who* stole him," Elizabeth continued. "We need to find some suspects who had motive and opportunity."

I was used to Elizabeth's detective talk. She meant we were looking for someone who had a reason to steal Tut and the chance to do it when no one was looking.

Unfortunately, we weren't going to be able to figure that out right away. The clock on the barn read 9:58. We had two minutes to get to the stables. And considering they were halfway across the farm, Elizabeth and I really had to hurry.

• • •

"Whoa! Hold it! STOP!"

We had been on the horse trail for about twenty minutes when I heard Mrs. Sloane yelling. I looked to my left and saw her horse take off into the woods with her still on him.

"Bucky's out of control," I heard one of the farmhands shout.

"I'll go get him," another farmhand answered.

"WHOA!" Mrs. Sloane shouted again.

"GET OFF MY BACK!" Mrs. Sloane's horse whinnied to her.

I was really glad Sasha couldn't understand horse-

talk. If she knew Mrs. Sloane's horse was complaining about taking her for a ride, Sasha would never let the rest of us hear the end of it.

But Sasha hadn't understood a thing. She was riding quietly along the trail, two horses ahead of me, with her long brown braid hanging out from under her riding helmet. She didn't even turn around when one of the farmhands hurried off to bring Mrs. Sloane and her horse back onto the trail.

"Roy must have really hated *that* two-legged one," my horse, Buttercup, suddenly whinnied to the horse in front of her.

"You're not kidding," the other horse replied. "He gave her Bucky to ride."

"Why do you say that?" I whispered into Buttercup's ear.

Buttercup stopped right where she was. She turned her head as far as she could to look at me. "Did you say something?" she whinnied nervously. I guess she'd never met a kid who could talk to horses before.

Just then, one of the farmhands rode up beside me. "Give Buttercup a kick," he told me. "That'll get her moving again."

"Sorry," I whispered in Buttercup's ear as I kicked her gently in the side. "He told me to do it."

"No problem," Buttercup whinnied back as she started to move along the trail again. "I'm used to it. It's a two-legged way of telling me to move. It's not like two-leggeds can talk to me. At least not usually. But you . . ."

"Yeah, I know," I said. "It's weird."

"But how?" Buttercup asked.

"It's a long story." One I didn't have time to tell. So instead, I just asked, "Why do you think Roy hates my teacher?"

"Bucky's a wild horse," Buttercup explained. "He gallops to his own beat. No *clip-clop, clip-clop* for him."

"More like *clip-clop-drop*," the horse in front of us whinnied cheerfully. "Sometimes Bucky throws people just for fun."

Uh-oh. Poor Mrs. Sloane.

"Roy is the head farmhand. He knows Bucky can be trouble," Buttercup told me. "He'd never give him to anyone he liked."

"But why wouldn't Roy like my teacher?" I asked Buttercup. "They just met today."

Buttercup shook her head back and forth. "I don't know. Roy doesn't like strangers coming to the farm."

"How can you tell?" I asked her.

"Horse sense, of course," Buttercup whinnied.

As we rode along the path, I thought about what Buttercup had said. It sounded like Roy would do just about anything to keep strangers away from the farm.

Maybe even kidnap a tortoise, just to get back at us for daring to visit.

Chapter 7

"I think I have a suspect," I whispered to Elizabeth as we got off our horses and led them to the water trough. I made sure we were far away from everyone else so we could talk about our detective stuff in private.

"Who?" Elizabeth asked excitedly.

"The head farmhand, Roy," I said. "He doesn't like when people visit the farm. I think he's trying to scare away visitors. That's why he gave Mrs. Sloane that wild horse."

"Her horse *was* wild," Elizabeth said. "It looked like he was trying to throw her off his back. But Mrs. Sloane held on."

"Mrs. Sloane was definitely impressive," I agreed.

Buttercup swished her tail up and down. "Darn flies!" she whinnied.

BZZZ

"Ouch!" I heard a small voice say. "What do you horses have against us flies, anyway?"

"Buzz off, Buzzy," Buttercup neighed.

"Who told you about Roy?" Elizabeth asked me.

"My horse," I replied, petting Buttercup on the head as she took a drink from the trough.

Elizabeth wasn't surprised. She was used to my unusual sources by now.

"Move over," Elizabeth's horse, Ladybug, scolded Buttercup. "You're hogging the water."

"I'm no hog!" Buttercup whinnied. "Do you see a curly pink tail on this rear end?"

I laughed. But I stopped laughing when I spotted Leo watching Elizabeth and me. As soon as he saw me, Leo turned and walked over to Roy.

I wanted to stop him. But I couldn't. How would I explain why I knew Roy didn't like visitors? I couldn't just say, "My horse told me."

"Can I brush my horse?" I heard Leo ask Roy.

"No," Roy answered gruffly. "You'll mess up his coat."

"Not if you teach me how to do it," Leo said.

"Fine, I'll show you," Roy grumbled. "But it's not easy to groom a horse. Look at those pictures on the barn wall. Those are our horses at shows. See how tightly braided their tails are? It takes a lot of time. Time I don't have because I'm babysitting you kids all day."

"Roy's nasty," Elizabeth said. "He really *could* be the tortoise kidnapper."

"I know," I said. "Should we interrogate him?"

Interrogate was another detective word Elizabeth had taught me. It means to ask a bunch of questions to find out if the suspect did the crime.

"Not yet," Elizabeth said. "We should be really sure before we talk to him."

I looked over at Roy. He was stomping around in his heavy cowboy boots. The guy had huge feet. He left massive, muddy footprints everywhere he walked.

Elizabeth was right. There was no point in accusing a guy like that of anything unless you were really certain. He could squash you like a bug.

Just then a fly landed right on my nose. I tried to shoo him away, but he wouldn't budge.

"Get lost, bug," I said.

"I prefer to be called *insect*," the fly said. "Or by my real name, Buzzy. You said something about a crime. Maybe I can help. I'm a detective."

I laughed. "Right. A fly detective."

"Exactly," Buzzy said. "And a good one. How many detectives do you know who have two hundred lenses in their eyes that can see in any direction?"

"What's the fly saying?" Elizabeth asked me.

"He wants to help," I said. "He's a detective."

"So, what are you looking for?" Buzzy asked me.

"Tut," I answered.

"What's a Tut?"

"My sister's tortoise," I said.

"What's a tortoise?" Buzzy flew onto my arm and started tiptoeing up to my elbow.

"Cut it out," I said. "That tickles."

"You humans are too easily distracted," Buzzy said. "If you want to solve a case, you must stick to the topic. Why don't you tell me where you last saw this Tut-tortoise thingamabob?"

"He was in the red barn," I said. "And now he's not."

Buzzy flew up to my ear. "You're in luck," he hummed. "I spent half the morning in the barn. If someone took something, I saw it happen."

"What's he saying *now*?" Elizabeth sounded tired of understanding only half the conversation.

"Buzzy was in the barn this morning," I explained. "He could be a witness."

"Great!" Elizabeth said. "Start interrogating him."

Sheesh. Did she think she was the only detective here?

"Did you see anyone suspicious in the barn?" I asked.

"It was pretty quiet," Buzzy buzzed. "Until that tall, scary human came by."

Whoa. Buzzy may have been all eyes, but suddenly I was all *ears*. I pointed across the stables to where

Roy was slamming our riding helmets back into a big trunk. "Was that the human you saw?" I asked.

"I don't know. I didn't see its face," Buzzy admitted. "All I know is the human was really angry. It stomped into the barn, grabbed something with its front legs, and stomped out."

I thought for a minute. Front legs? That didn't make any sense. But then I remembered that flies only have legs. Buzzy must have meant hands.

"What did this person take?" I asked the fly.

"I'm not sure," he admitted. "It came out of a box on a shelf near the haystack."

Tut's box!

"You're absolutely sure?" I asked him.

"Definitely," the fly said. "I told you. I never miss a thing." He did a loop-the-loop in the air.

"Wow!" I exclaimed. "Awesome!"

"That's nothing," Buzzy said. "You should see my triple flip."

"Not your trick," I said. "What you just said."

"*What* did he say?" Elizabeth asked excitedly.

"Buzzy just gave us a clue!" I told her. "And it's a whopper!"

Chapter 8

"Why are we going back to the red barn again?" I asked Elizabeth a few minutes later.

"For one thing, Mrs. Sloane said we had to see the sheep-shearing demonstration, and they're going to do that there," Elizabeth explained. "For another, we need to see if the person Buzzy spotted in the barn left any evidence behind."

"Then let's hurry," I said. "The last thing I need is to be in trouble with Mrs. Sloane. I'm going to be in enough trouble later if I come home without Tut."

"That won't happen," Elizabeth said. She sounded really sure about it.

That made one of us.

• • •

The first thing we heard when we got to the barn was Sasha. She was arguing with a farmhand . . . again.

"Has anyone asked if this sheep wants a haircut?" Sasha asked. "I know I wouldn't want anyone cutting off my braid without asking me!"

The kids all laughed. They thought Sasha was nuts. You could tell by the way they were rolling their eyes. Trevor was even wiggling his finger around in a circle near his ear, which is the sign for crazy.

But the thing is, Sasha actually wasn't crazy (for once!). That sheep was definitely complaining.

"Talk about a *baaaaad* hair day," he groaned. "I asked the *baaa*rber to take a little off the top. But instead he's giving me this buzz cut!"

I wanted to start looking for evidence. But before I could, Leo walked over to Elizabeth and me.

"Where have you been, Jack?" he asked.

"Um . . . uh . . ." I stammered. "We got lost coming back from the stables."

I hated lying to my best friend. But what was I supposed to say? "I was talking to a fly about a tortoise"?

"You still solving your mystery?" Leo asked.

"Yeah," I said. "But—"

"I'll leave you guys alone." Leo turned and walked back to the other kids. He looked really bummed.

"He'll get over it," Elizabeth said. "But Mia won't if you don't find Tut."

She was right . . . as usual.

"Tell me again what Buzzy told you," Elizabeth said.

"He saw a tall human come into the barn, take something from the box, and leave," I said. "It must have been Roy. He's taller than the other farmhands."

"He's tall, all right," Elizabeth agreed. "But it doesn't mean he's the thief."

"Why not?" I asked her.

"You have to think like a fly," Elizabeth told me. "Flies are tiny. Humans *all* look big to them."

I frowned. She was right, again. Although . . .

"Buzzy said this person seemed really angry and was stomping all around," I remembered aloud.

"Now *that's* a good clue." Elizabeth wrote the words *angry* and *stomping* in her notebook. "Stomping," she said quietly. Then she walked over to where Tut's box was perched on the shelf.

"What are you doing?" I asked.

"I'm hunting for a clue." She looked down at the ground.

I looked down, too. Only, I had no idea what I was looking for.

"Well, that settles it," Elizabeth said finally.

"*What* settles it?" I asked her.

"Roy's not the thief," she told me.

"Of course he is," I said. "He fits all the descriptions Buzzy gave us."

"Not all," Elizabeth disagreed. "Look at these footprints."

I looked down. All I saw were a bunch of sneaker prints. "So?" I said. "We're all wearing sneakers. Mrs. Sloane told us to wear sneakers because we were going to be walking a lot."

"That's just it," Elizabeth said. "Most of the kids here are wearing sneakers. But Roy isn't. He's wearing cowboy boots. *Big*, muddy cowboy boots. I don't see giant boot prints anywhere."

Wow. Impressive. We didn't call Elizabeth the Brainiac for nothing. She was one smart detective.

But without Roy, Elizabeth and I were out of suspects. That sheep wasn't the only one having a *baaa*d day.

Chapter 9

Elizabeth didn't look happy. But she wasn't giving up. As soon as the sheep shearing was over, she raced out of the barn to find new clues. I followed.

"Maybe one of the other animals saw something," Elizabeth whispered. "Like that pony over there."

I looked in the direction Elizabeth was pointing to see a small, chocolate brown pony nibbling on some oats. Her job was to give rides to any little kids who came to the farm. But since we were big kids, she wasn't busy. So while the rest of the third graders went off to learn about growing corn, Elizabeth and I snuck over to talk to the pony.

"Excuse me," I said to her.

"You're too big," the pony neighed without even looking up. "No one taller than three feet gets a ride." She went back to chewing.

"I don't want a ride," I said. "I want to know if you saw anyone carrying a tortoise today."

"Carrying a *what*?" the pony asked me.

"A tortoise," I repeated. "You know, with a shell?"

"What's a shell?" the pony asked.

"This is hopeless," I told Elizabeth.

Elizabeth was about to put her pen away when the pony started neighing again.

"I did see someone go by," she told me. "A two-legged animal. But it was holding a rock, not a . . . what did you call that thing again?"

"Tortoise," I repeated.

"What's she saying?" Elizabeth asked me.

"Nothing we can use," I answered. "Something about someone walking by with a rock."

"A rock, huh?" Elizabeth began to smile. "Ask her to describe the rock."

I couldn't figure out what help that would be. But it seemed really important to Elizabeth. So I asked, "What did the rock look like?"

"It was kind of greenish brown." The pony looked up for a minute and thought. "And there was something weird about it. There were moving parts."

PONY RIDES
CLOSED

"Moving parts?" I repeated.

"Well, it was like it had legs and a tail. I think I saw a head, but then it disappeared," the pony said. "That's strange for a rock, don't you think?"

I began to smile. That rock sounded a whole lot like a tortoise to me! They stick their heads out of their shells, and then pull them right back in again—especially if they're scared.

"She saw someone with the tortoise!" I said excitedly.

"Great," Elizabeth said. "Can she describe the person?"

Oh yeah. That *would* help.

"What did the person who was carrying the tort—I mean the *rock*—look like?" I asked the pony.

"About your height," the pony whinnied. "And wearing a hat."

Oh man. That could be anyone in the third grade.

"The human was ready for a show," the pony continued. "I could tell because of its tail."

I shook my head at Elizabeth. "This pony is nuts."

"Excuse *you*?" the pony said. "You asked a question and I answered. You don't have to be mean."

Oops. I'd forgotten the pony could understand me even when I wasn't talking to her.

“I’m sorry,” I said. “Thanks for your help.”

As Elizabeth and I walked away, I whispered, “You’re not going to believe this.”

“What?” Elizabeth asked.

“She said the person carrying Tut was going to a horse show,” I explained. “She could tell because of its tail. What kind of person has a tail?”

“I don’t know,” Elizabeth admitted. “But we’ll figure it out. We just have to think like a pony.”

Suddenly, I heard a loud gurgling noise. But it wasn’t coming from an animal. It was my stomach.

“Let’s go to the picnic area,” I told Elizabeth. “I’ll think better on a full stomach.”

Not that I really believed that. I could eat all day long and I’d probably never figure out which of us third graders was actually hiding a tail. I didn’t believe that kind of person even existed.

But up until a few weeks before, I hadn’t believed people could talk to animals, either. So anything was possible. *Anything.*

Chapter 10

Leo was sitting by himself near a tree when Elizabeth and I got to the picnic area.

"Where have you been?" he asked me angrily. "You keep disappearing."

"We've been trying to find Tut," I explained as I took out my peanut butter and jelly sandwich.

"Whatever," Leo grumbled. He went back to eating his cheese sandwich.

"Um . . . Jack . . . can I talk to you for a minute?" Elizabeth asked. She looked over at Leo. "In *private,*" she added.

"Go ahead," Leo told me. "Your *partner* is calling you."

The way Leo said *partner* sounded a lot like Trevor the Terrible—especially when he called Elizabeth and me kissy faces. That made me feel even more rotten, which I didn't think was possible.

"Leo's really mad at you," Elizabeth said as soon as we were alone.

Duh. "You think?" I asked her sarcastically.

"He was mad when you found Tut in your backpack, too, wasn't he?" Elizabeth asked.

"Yeah," I said. "We were both mad at Mia."

"No," Elizabeth corrected me. "*You* were mad at Mia. Leo was mad that you had a tortoise in your backpack. Do you think he was mad enough to take the tortoise?"

"That's ridiculous," I said. "Leo's my best friend."

"*And* your field-trip buddy," Elizabeth agreed. "He was really looking forward to this trip. Do you think he was worried having Tut here would ruin things?"

I thought about that. Leo had been kind of upset when I said I was worried about leaving Tut behind. But that didn't mean anything.

"That can't be right," I said. "Now that Tut's missing, Leo's having an even worse time."

"Maybe he didn't think ahead about what would happen *after* he took Tut," Elizabeth said. "Lots of people don't think about stuff like that—especially when they're angry."

I frowned. Elizabeth wasn't one of those people. She always thought of everything. So she was kind of saying Leo wasn't as smart as her—without actually saying it. Sometimes the Brainiac could be a real *Pain*iac.

Which was why I was doubly happy to be able to prove to her that she was wrong. "Why isn't he giving Tut back now then?" I asked.

"Because he's madder than ever," Elizabeth said. "He gets jealous when we work on a case together."

That was true, even though I didn't like hearing Elizabeth say it out loud.

But deep down, I knew Leo would never steal Tut. No matter how mad he was, Leo was no crook.

"It can't be him. He doesn't have a tail," I pointed out.

"No," Elizabeth agreed. "But he does have a keychain collection hanging from his backpack. That could sort of look like a tail—to an animal, anyway."

Man, she was smart.

"Think, Jack," Elizabeth asked me. "Were you and Leo ever apart before Tut disappeared?"

"Well, he did go to the bathroom just before we went to the reptile room," I said slowly.

Then I frowned, remembering what Leo had said just before we separated for those few minutes: *Sounds like a plan. It's always important to have a plan.*

I gulped. Could Leo's plan have been to kidnap Tut?

"I think we need to ask Leo a few questions," Elizabeth said.

"Um . . . maybe we need to find a few more clues to see if there's anyone else who could have done it," I suggested.

"You're stalling," Elizabeth said. "You don't want to interrogate Leo."

Now I wasn't just hungry. I was mad. But not at Leo. At *Elizabeth*. She just didn't get it. "That's right," I told her angrily. "I don't want to accuse my best friend of doing something this mean. Especially because *I don't think he did it*!"

Elizabeth stared at me and twirled one of her red, wormy hair curls around her finger. I thought she was going to cry.

But instead she said, "Okay. Go talk to more animals. See what they tell you. And then, when you find out that I'm right, talk to Leo."

I can't stand when Elizabeth acts like a know-it-all—even though she does pretty much know it all.

But she was wrong this time. It couldn't be Leo. No way.

Or could it?

Chapter 11

I had to prove Elizabeth wrong. I had to find someone who might have seen the person who stole Tut. So while everyone else ate their lunches, I searched for someone who could clear my friend.

The petting zoo was close to the barn, the bathroom, and the reptile room. If Leo had passed by with Mia's tortoise, one of the baby animals might have seen him. But I really hoped they hadn't.

"You want to play tag?"

As I stepped into the petting zoo, a small voice called up to me from the ground. I looked down. There were three yellow baby chicks.

"We love tag," one chick told me.

"It's our favorite game," another added.

“Tag! You’re it!” The third chick pecked at my leg and ran off.

“Come on,” the first chick said. “You’ve been tagged. Now you run. That’s the game.”

“I’m not here to play,” I said. “I’m trying to find out if my friend passed by here today. Maybe you saw him. He’s smaller than me, with curly hair, and—”

“Does he play tag?” the first chick asked. (At least I *thought* it was the first chick. It was hard to tell because they kept moving around.)

“Tag! You’re it!” a chick said.

“No, *you’re* it!” another chick shouted, pecking him back.

I frowned. There was no way these chicks were going to be any help.

But I wasn't giving up. I had to talk to someone—*anyone*—in the petting zoo who might be able to clear my best friend's name. This was one time I really, *really* wanted the Brainiac to be wrong.

"Excuse me," I said to a goat who was sticking his nose through the gate, trying to reach the garbage can. "Can I ask you something?"

"What?" the goat asked. He nudged his nose toward my backpack.

I knew exactly what he was up to. I also knew it wasn't going to do him any good. My lunch wasn't in my backpack anymore.

"I don't have any food," I told him.

The goat pulled his head back. "Bummer. That one kid had a tuna sandwich."

"Kid?" I asked. "You mean like a baby goat?"

"No, I mean a kid like you," he said. "We're both kids, aren't we?"

I'd never thought of it like that. "I guess so," I said.

"That's why I didn't feel bad about taking that

tuna sandwich," the goat continued. "When it comes to us kids, it's share and share alike."

"Tuna sandwich?" I repeated.

The goat nodded. "It wasn't very good. Really stale. I think it was in the backpack for a long time."

Oh no. That was bad. *Really* bad. Leo always left part of his lunch in his backpack. Sometimes for days. One time I saw him pull out a piece of bread that was so old it had purple and blue mold growing all over it.

"Did you happen to notice if the kid with the sandwich was carrying anything?" I asked. "Like maybe a rock with a head and four legs?"

The goat looked at me like I was crazy. "There's no rock like that," he told me.

"But the pony said . . ." I began. Then I stopped. "Oh, never mind."

"This kid *was* carrying something, I think," the goat said. "But it was under his shirt. I couldn't tell what it was. He seemed kind of nervous, too. His eyes were darting all around."

I wasn't surprised. The thing under his shirt had probably been a tortoise. And a thief would be nervous. *Really* nervous.

"There was something weird," the goat continued. "You two-leggeds have a very distinct smell. But so do horses. And this kid smelled like a horse."

A kid who smelled like a horse. Oh man. Leo had been brushing his horse at the stable. That would make him smell like a horse. Which meant Elizabeth was right. All the clues pointed to one person. My best friend, Leo.

Make that my soon-to-be *ex*–best friend.

Elizabeth was waiting for me at the edge of the picnic area when I got back.

“So?” she asked.

I frowned. “You were right,” I said. “Leo’s the tortoise-napper.” I filled her in on all the clues the goat had given me.

I figured Elizabeth would act all know-it-all when I told her she was right. But she didn’t. In fact, she looked kind of sad.

“I’m sorry,” she said. “I was almost hoping I was wrong.”

So was I. And not almost.

But Elizabeth *wasn’t* wrong. And now I had to accuse my best friend of stealing Mia’s tortoise.

“Let’s go talk to him,” Elizabeth said.

“No,” I told her. “I’ll do this alone. I’ll meet you back at the barn when I’m done.”

Elizabeth gave me a funny look. “Are you sure?”

I wasn’t sure of anything—except that I didn’t want Elizabeth getting all detective-like with Leo. That would just make him madder. I wanted to interrogate him my way.

Unfortunately, I had no idea what *my way* was. I was just going to have to make it up as I went along.

Chapter 12

"Hey, Leo." I sat down next to him beneath a big, shady tree at the far end of the picnic area. Most of the other kids were sitting in groups. But not Leo.

"Nice of you to come back," Leo said. "I had to eat lunch all by myself."

Which you wouldn't have had to do if you hadn't stolen Mia's tortoise, I thought. But out loud I just said, "I was looking for clues. It takes time to solve a mystery."

"So you solved it?" Leo asked. He looked down at the ground.

Wow. He couldn't even look me in the eye. You didn't have to be a Brainiac to know that was how a guilty guy acted.

"I think so," I said. "It was someone who was really mad about Tut being here."

"Like you," Leo pointed out.

"Or *you*," I said. Well, actually, I kind of mumbled it under my breath.

But Leo heard me. Loud and clear. And if he was mad before, he was *furious* now.

"YOU THINK *I* STOLE TUT?" he shouted at the top of his lungs.

"Well, you had motive," I said. "And opportunity. And the goat—I mean *someone*—saw you hiding something under your shirt when you were near the petting zoo."

"Yeah. I was hiding my worksheet," Leo said. "Trevor was there. I didn't want to have to give him my answers. You know how he always wants to copy."

Then things got a lot worse. Trevor popped out from behind the other side of the tree. I hadn't noticed him there. I never would have said anything about Leo stealing Tut if I knew Trevor would hear me.

But he *had* heard me.

"You're a sorry excuse for a best friend!" Trevor told me. "How can you accuse your buddy of being a thief?"

"Yeah!" Leo agreed.

"Jack and his kissy-face girlfriend accused me of being a thief once, too," Trevor told Leo. "They thought I stole your homework for the science fair. They were wrong then . . ."

"And they're wrong now," Leo added.

Oh boy. This was bad. Now Leo and Trevor were on the same side. I was too upset to even remind Trevor that Elizabeth wasn't my kissy-face girlfriend. I was too upset to say *anything.*

"So, Leo, did you get the answer to question eight?" Trevor asked. "The one about why males turkeys spread their tail feathers?"

I waited for Leo to tell Trevor to do his own work. But that's not what happened. Instead, Leo pulled his worksheet out of his backpack.

"Here you go," he said to Trevor. "Just make sure *Jack* doesn't copy from it. He missed the turkey talk because he was working on his dumb old mystery."

As Trevor and Leo walked away, I wanted to shout out that I didn't need Leo's answers. I could just ask the turkeys myself.

But I didn't say that. Now was definitely not the time to tell Leo about my special talent.

I raced over to the red barn to find Elizabeth. Unfortunately, I didn't have much to tell her. It wasn't like Leo had confessed or anything.

Elizabeth ran up to the barn door just as I arrived. Her face was all red and sweaty. "Jack!" she shouted. "Have you talked to Leo yet?"

"Yeah," I said. "And he denies everything."

"That's because he didn't do it," Elizabeth explained.

"WHAT?!" I yelled. "But you said . . ."

"I know," Elizabeth said. "I *thought* he was the thief. But I studied the clues, and . . . well . . . Leo can't be the one who took Tut."

"ARE YOU KIDDING ME?" I shouted.

"I didn't think of this before," Elizabeth admitted. "But the goat said that when he took the tuna sandwich out of the kid's backpack, the kid smelled like a horse."

"Tell me something I don't know," I said. I knew I was being mean, but I couldn't help it. Elizabeth had just made me accuse my best friend of being a thief!

"The smell of horses had to come *after* we went horseback riding," Elizabeth explained. "But Tut was already missing by then."

I stared at her. It was such as an easy thing. How could she have missed it?

Of course I had missed it, too. But *I'm* not a genius.

"I wish you had pointed that out before," I told her.

"Me too," Elizabeth admitted.

"This whole day has been so weird," I told her.

"I know," Elizabeth agreed. "But once we solve this case, everything will go back to normal."

Back to normal? So far today I'd spoken to Scout, a snake, a cow, some horses, a fly, a sheep, three chicks, and a goat. There was nothing normal about this field trip. *At least not for me.*

Chapter 13

"Leo, we're *really* sorry," I told him for about the eighth time. Elizabeth and I had run back to the picnic area and were now sitting with Leo at one of the tables. It was almost the end of lunch, and I still hadn't eaten. But I figured this was more important than food.

"I can't believe you accused me of stealing Mia's tortoise," Leo said.

"Everyone makes mistakes sometimes—even detectives," Elizabeth told him.

"Yeah," I agreed. "Remember, you accused Scout of stealing your homework, and he didn't do it."

"That's different," Leo said. "Scout's a dog."

"Dogs have feelings, too," I told him. "Trust me."

Leo shook his head. "I can't believe I let Trevor copy my worksheet."

"He would have gotten it from you eventually," I told Leo. "He just didn't have to work as hard."

Leo nodded. Trevor always got what he wanted—usually by just being Trevor the Terrible. Leo reached into his bag. "My mom gave me chocolate chip cookies for dessert. You want one?"

I smiled. Our fight was over. "Sure," I said. "Thanks."

"Do you guys have any other suspects?" Leo asked.

My smile became a frown. "Not yet."

"But we will," Elizabeth promised.

I wasn't so sure. The field trip was more than half over, and still no Tut.

Just then, Sasha jumped up from a nearby picnic table and began swatting at some bugs. "There are so many flies at this farm!" she shouted.

Suddenly, I wasn't focused on my problems. My attention was on Sasha. Everyone's was. She was so loud and angry.

"Can't they do anything about all the bugs?" Sasha's long braid swung back and forth as she tried to shoo the flies away from her sandwich.

Leo laughed. "Sasha's hilarious," he said.

But Elizabeth wasn't laughing. She was staring at her notebook. Suddenly, she gasped.

"THE TAIL!" she exclaimed.

Leo and I both stared at her. Neither of us had any idea what she was talking about. Sometimes it seemed like the Brainiac was talking in code.

"In the pictures on the barn wall, all the show horses had their tails braided," Elizabeth reminded me.

Now it was my turn to smile. I knew exactly what Elizabeth meant. There *was* someone in our class who fit the description the horse had given me.

"A tail on the *head,*" I muttered. "A braided ponytail."

"Exactly," Elizabeth said with a grin.

"What are you two talking about?" Leo asked us.

"Um . . . Leo, do you mind if we go do some mystery work?" I asked him.

"More?" he asked. "Why don't you give up already?"

"Come on, Leo," I said. "You'd want me to find Mr. Sniffles if *he* was missing."

"Yeah," Leo admitted. "I guess even Mia the Pain deserves to get her tortoise back."

"It won't take long," Elizabeth told him. "I think we've finally got this case solved."

AH-HA!
SHOO!!!

Chapter 14

One minute later, the Brainiac and I were standing in front of Sasha.

"Where's Tut?" Elizabeth demanded.

"Where's *what*?" Sasha asked. But I could tell by the way she was nervously biting her lip and looking away that she knew *exactly* what we meant.

"My sister's tortoise," I said. "You stole him."

Sasha stuck her chin in the air and began to play with her long brown braid. "I didn't *steal* anything," she said.

"Are you trying to tell us that you have no idea where that tortoise is?" Elizabeth demanded.

"I didn't say that," Sasha said.

"What's that supposed to mean?" I asked her.

"You and your sister were holding that tortoise prisoner," Sasha told me.

Elizabeth rolled her eyes. "Just answer the question, Sasha," she said, sounding a lot like a real detective. "Did you take the tortoise out of the barn?"

"He wanted me to," Sasha said. "But I didn't steal him. I said his name and he started to follow me. That's not stealing."

Now it was *my* turn to sound like a real detective, because I knew Sasha was lying.

"There's no way he followed you," I told Sasha. "Tut would never come when you called his name."

"How do you know?" Sasha said. "You weren't there."

"No, but I know a lot about tortoises," I told her. "My sister has all kind of books about them. I read them to her sometimes."

Elizabeth looked surprised. "You read to Mia?" she asked me.

"Only when my parents make me," I admitted. "But that's how I know about tortoises. They can barely hear, if at all. Hearing is their weakest sense. So where's the tortoise that you *stole*?"

"You mean the tortoise I *freed*," Sasha insisted. "There's no way I'm telling you where he is."

"You have to tell us, Sasha," Elizabeth pleaded. "Tut could be in big trouble."

"He's fine," Sasha said. "He's in a place with lots of grass and clover to eat."

"But . . ." I didn't know what to say after that. I'd been so focused on finding out who the thief was, I'd never considered what Elizabeth and I would do if the thief refused to give Tut back.

"What's going on here?" Mrs. Sloane asked as she made her way over to Sasha's picnic table. "Trevor told me you kids were arguing."

Ordinarily, I would be angry that Trevor had tattled on us. But right now I was more angry with Sasha.

"Sasha took Mia's tortoise," I said.

Mrs. Sloane looked at Sasha with surprise. "Is that true?" she asked her.

Sasha folded her arms across her chest. "I didn't take him. I *freed* him."

Now even Mrs. Sloane looked worried.

"He's fine," Sasha told Mrs. Sloane. "He's got plenty of food. And it's nice and warm out. Just like in a desert."

"It's nice and warm now," I told her. "But it's not going to be warm tonight. If it gets too cold, Tut could get sick . . . or worse!"

"What are you talking about?" Sasha asked me nervously.

"Tut could die because the night is cooler than the day, and he needs to be in a warm environment," I said, remembering what I had read in Mia's tortoise books. "His tank in Mia's room has a heater that's on all day and night. And she feeds him special tortoise food, so what he eats is healthy for him."

Sasha looked at me. "But your sister stuck her tortoise in your backpack. That couldn't have been healthy."

She had a point there.

"That's true," I agreed. "But Mia only did it because she loves Tut and she wanted him to have an adventure."

I couldn't believe I was saying that. I also couldn't believe I meant it. Mia really did love Tut. And she took good care of him—*usually*.

"He has definitely had an adventure," Mrs. Sloane agreed. She looked sternly at Sasha. "Now tell us where you put the tortoise."

Sasha had no choice, and she knew it.

"He's over by the big tree," she said, pointing to a tree not far from where we were picnicking. "At least, that's where I left him this morning."

"It's too bad animals can't talk," Leo said. "Then we could just shout out his name, and he could tell us where he was."

Elizabeth and I looked at each other.

This was a big farm, and Tut could be anywhere. Finding him was going to be like looking for a tortoise in a haystack. And that's never easy.

Chapter 15

I didn't see Tut at first. All I saw was a lot of green grass, and a few leaves. But no tortoise.

And then, my ears took over.

BURP! The first thing I heard was a loud belch.

"Aah, that's better," I heard a slow voice say. "Boy, this all-you-can-eat buffet is amazing."

All-you-can-eat buffet? *Huh?*

"I wish they had something other than grass and clover," the voice said. "Maybe an apple slice, or a carrot. Tortoises like carrots."

Tortoises! That had to be Tut talking. And he was pretty loud, so he had to be nearby.

"Careful with your feet!" I called out. "I have a feeling Tut's real close."

I looked down at the ground. Sure enough, just a few

inches from where I was standing, I saw something green and brown. It looked kind of like a rock—except it had legs, a head, and a tail. *Exactly the way the pony had described it.*

"I've got him," I shouted. Then I bent down and lifted Tut off the ground.

"Hey, I haven't had dessert yet," he said.

I laughed. All the animals on this farm had pretty much the same thing on their minds. Food.

Grrrrummmmble . . . Suddenly, my stomach started to growl. I hadn't eaten a thing since breakfast. Food was pretty much the only thing on my mind, too.

"Do I still have time to eat my sandwich?" I asked Mrs. Sloane.

She nodded. "Why don't you give Tut to me?" she suggested, taking the tortoise from my hands. "I'll watch him. Then you and your friends can finish lunch and enjoy the rest of the day."

"Thanks," I said. Then we kids started to walk toward the picnic area.

"Wait a minute," Mrs. Sloane called.

We all stopped and turned around. *What now?*

"Sasha," Mrs. Sloane said, "you're not going anywhere. You and I need to have a *long* chat!"

For the first time ever, Sasha didn't have anything to say. Which was okay, because I didn't think Mrs. Sloane was going to let her do much talking, anyway.

"I wonder if Tut was scared out there, all alone and so far from home," Leo asked me.

I laughed. "Nah. He was never far from home," I said.

"What are you talking about?" Leo asked. "This place is an hour away from your house."

"Yeah, but remember, Tut's a tortoise," I said. "So he's always home. A tortoise carries his home on his back!"

"And now you'll be able to get him *back home*," Elizabeth added with a grin. "Safe and sound."

The field trip was a lot more fun after that. Even Roy didn't seem so scary anymore. Especially as I watched him trying to give a bunch of baby piglets a bath.

"GET OVER HERE NOW, YOU SQUIRMING SQUEAKERS!" Roy shouted. He sloshed around in the mud, trying to catch the pink piglets.

"I hate bath time!" the pig squealed back.

To everyone else it just sounded like *squeak squeal squeak*, but I heard that piglet loud and clear.

"It looks like Roy could use some help," Mrs. Sloane suggested.

Trevor shot our teacher a fake smile. "I'll help him. How hard can it be to catch a baby pig?"

Pretty hard, I thought. But I didn't say that. I just watched Trevor step into the pigsty.

"You can't catch me!" the piglet squealed.

Trevor reached for the squealing pig, and . . . *splat!* He fell face-first into the mud!

Leo, Elizabeth, and I totally cracked up. Trevor shot

us a really angry look—but that just made us laugh harder.

A pig raced by. Roy was right behind him. "I got you!" Roy shouted. And then . . .

Splat! Roy tripped over Trevor and landed in the mud.

"Dumb kids," Roy grumbled.

"Missed me, missed me, now you gotta kiss me!" the piglet squealed.

Just then Buzzy the fly landed on my shoulder. "Hey, Jack," he said. "Did you solve the mystery?"

“Yep,” I answered. “Thanks.”

“Good. Because I’m leaving the detective biz,” Buzzy told me. “I’m going to be a comic.”

I’d never heard of a fly comic before. Then again, before today I’d never heard of a fly detective, either.

“Why did the fly fly?” Buzzy joked.

“Why?” I asked.

“Because the spider spied ’er,” he answered.

I started to laugh.

“Hey! You better not be laughing at me!” Trevor shouted out suddenly.

Gulp. I was definitely not laughing at Trevor. But I wasn’t going to tell him what I *was* laughing at. My whole talking-to-animals thing was going to stay a mystery to everyone except the Brainiac and me.

Which makes sense. After all, mysteries are our specialty.

CALLING ALL DETECTIVES!

Be sure to read all the Jack Gets a Clue mysteries!

Here's a sneak peek of

The Case of the Green Guinea Pig . . .

Leo and I were about halfway down the hall when we suddenly heard a loud scream. It was coming from the end of the hall.

I turned around and saw Nurse Kauffman standing in the doorway of the first aid room. She was covered in white confetti.

We both started laughing. She looked like an abominable snow nurse.

Principal Bumble hurried over to the first aid room. "What happened here?" she asked.

"Someone put a bucket of confetti up there." Nurse Kauffman spit a piece of white confetti out of her mouth and pointed to the top of her doorframe. "When I opened the door, the bucket tipped over, and it all poured down on me." She looked down at the floor. "What a mess. I'll have to call Mr. Broomfield to clean up. He's not going to be happy."

I knew what Nurse Kauffman meant. Mr. Broomfield was the school janitor. He was a big grump on a good day. The extra work cleaning up the first aid room would make him even more miserable.

Principal Bumble headed back to her office. A

moment later, we all heard her voice ring out over the PA system.

"It seems we have a prankster in our school today," Principal Bumble said. "I fully expect the person responsible for the pranks to stop immediately. We can't have someone running around playing tricks in school. If this continues, I will be forced to cancel the upper school apple-picking trip. If I can't trust you to behave here at school, how can I trust you to behave at the apple orchard?"

Cancel the field trip? No way! Sure, the pranks had been kind of funny. But no one was laughing now.